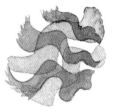

For Margaret O'Kelly who taught me how to teach the children
of Wonderland Nursery School, Hollywood, California—*J.N.H.*

For Margaret Crowden, a wonderful teacher—*J.N.H. and S.P.*

This edition first published in the United States in 2002 by MONDO Publishing,
by arrangement with Frances Lincoln Limited. Copyright © Frances Lincoln 2001.
Text copyright © Jana Novotny Hunter 2001.
Illustrations © Sue Porter 2001.

For information contact:
MONDO Publishing, 980 Avenue of the Americas, New York, NY 10018
Visit our web site at http://www.mondopub.com

Printed in Singapore
First MONDO printing 2002
ISBN 1-59034-196-1 (HC)   ISBN 1-59034-193-7 (PB)
09 9 8 7 6 5 4 3

I HAVE FEELINGS! was originally edited, designed and produced
by Frances Lincoln Limited, 4 Torriano Mews, Torriano Avenue, London NW5 2RZ.

Special Educational Edition only to be sold as a part of the "Bookshop" reading program.

Library of Congress Cataloging-in-Publication Data

Hunter, Jana Novotny.
   I have feelings / Jana Novotny Hunter ; illustrated by Sue Porter.
      p. cm.
   Summary: A mouse describes the feelings he and his family members experience
during the day, including feeling happy, sad, jealous, angry, and scared.
      ISBN 1-59034-961-1 (hc.) -- ISBN 1-59034-193-7 (pbk.)
      [1. Emotions--Fiction. 2. Mice--Fiction] I. Porter, Sue, ill. II. Title.

PZ7.H9168 Iae 2002
[E]--dc21   2002023525

I Have Feelings!

Jana Novotny Hunter

Illustrated by Sue Porter

Everybody has feelings.
Moms, dads, children, too,
and yes, even baby sisters do!
We all have feelings...

...even me and you.

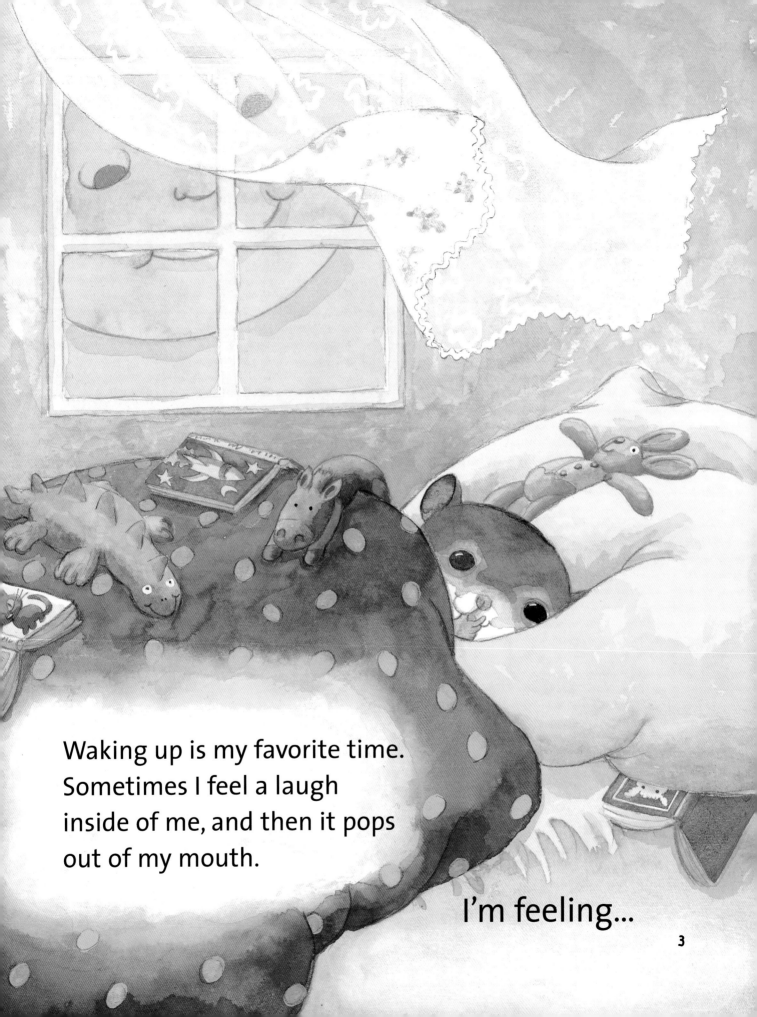

Waking up is my favorite time. Sometimes I feel a laugh inside of me, and then it pops out of my mouth.

I'm feeling...

happy!

Uh-oh! Someone's not happy now.
My baby sister feels full of tears.
She needs to cry them out.

My baby sister's feeling...

sad.

6

"Do you want to watch me dress myself?" I ask my baby sister.

"Look, I can put on
my own socks.
I can button my buttons
all by myself, too!"

I'm feeling...

7

proud.

8

Now that I'm dressed
we can go to the park.
"Hurry up, Mom!

Hurry up!"

I'm feeling speedy-fast inside.
I can't stop jumping.

I'm so...

9

excited!

But the excited feeling
goes away when my baby sister
gets to the big swing first.

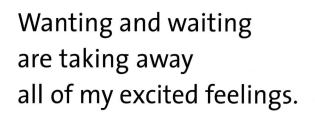

Wanting and waiting
are taking away
all of my excited feelings.

Now I'm feeling...

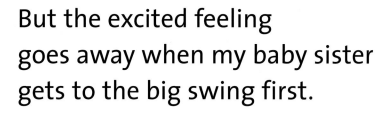

It's hard to share sometimes.
Anyway, my baby sister
is too little for that swing,
so I have to help her.

Helping her makes
me like myself.

I'm feeling...

kind.

"It's time to go home now!"
says Mom.

I have a shout inside of me.
I have to open my mouth and
let that shout out.
"No! I don't want to!
I don't want to!"

I'm feeling very...

Letting out the shout
helps the anger go away.
So when we get home
I feel better.

But at bedtime I get all
worried inside. I feel like
monsters are coming.

They're making me feel so...

My dad helps me chase
those monsters away.

I can feel a cuddle
coming down my arms.

I snuggle up and
give it to my dad.

I'm feeling...

love.

And Dad feels love right back!

Everybody has feelings.
Moms, dads, children, too,
and yes, even baby sisters do!
We all have feelings...

...even me and you.

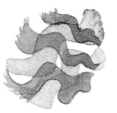